A MYTHIC LIFE

POEMS

JOHN MATTHEWS

APOCRYPHILE
PRESS

Apocryphile Press
PO Box 255
Hannacroix, NY 12087
www.apocryphilepress.com

Cover: "Story of Theseus" by Master of Cassoni (1406-1480).
Licensed from alamy.com.

Please join our mailing list at www.apocryphilepress.com/free. We'll keep you
up-to—date on all our new releases, and we'll also send you a FREE BOOK.
Visit us today!

CONTENTS

PART THREE
IN MYTH'S GREAT HEART

To Caitlín, always and forever,
for never faltering in your belief in me
and always acknowledging what I have achieved.

ACKNOWLEDGMENTS

Some of these poems have appeared in the following journals: *Temenos Review, Poetry London, Times Literary Supplement, Agenda, Labrys, The London Magazine.* There must be more which I have forgotten, so I thank all the editors here who accepted my work, especially Grahaeme Barrasford Young, William Cookson, Kathleen Raine, Tambimuttu and Steven O'Brien.

INTRODUCTION

I have written poetry throughout my life—from the first, generally horrible ramblings of teenage love, to the ramblings of one who has lived a long life.

Though I have published a number of these in a variety of magazines and journals, and even received a poetic blessing of one of my own most favoured masters, Robert Graves, it is only now that I have contemplated making a collection of these writings. Throughout all of this time, a single thread has connected everything that I have written, both in poetry and in prose, in fiction and in nonfiction—and that is myth. Myth, as the classical philosopher Sallustius memorably wrote, *is something which may never have happened, but is happening right now.* This seems to me a perfect metaphor for poetry which originates within a place between the worlds, between past and future, between present and never.

Inevitably, there are a number of poems which were generated by my lifelong love for the Arthurian myths and legends, some inspired by another much admired poet, Charles Williams, others simply emerging from within the great tangled forest that Dante knew so well, and in which I have spent so much of my life wandering, mostly lost, amid the wilderness of wonders and strange things.

So this collection represents almost sixty years of wandering and wondering, highlighting the things that have haunted me or spoken to me from amid the maelstrom of other writing executed in that time. There are still many more poems which I hope to publish in another collection, depending to a great degree on how this one is received. If people want more I have them. A much larger collection may therefore follow in due course if all comes about as I would wish.

John Matthews
Oxford, 2025

PART ONE
IN MYTH'S HOUSE
OF SHADOW

MYTHMAKER

You are the Mythmaker;
you it is who winds the maze
around my head—
putting out my eyes
with your fingers,
smothering me
in your hair.

You are the Mazemaker;
you it is who sends me wandering
lost in the twined convolutions
of our sudden-single mind,
caught in the meshes of our dream.

Your hands wind the myth in the mazes
of our deliberate unbelief;
your eyes blind me with their light;
your thought is dagger sharp
—a thin sliver of steel,
slipped beneath the lid

of my sarcophagus skull

With you I forget tomorrow
and the impossible fact of your absence;
you are the Mythmaker,
wrapping me in your rainbow winding-sheet
till I pass into your garden through the dark.

APOLLO AT DELPHI

In the sun's eye,
The scorpion cocks his tail to strike,
Hammers, again and again, at the air,
Feeling the movement of the gods
In the still heat of noon.

Silence shimmers on the hot stones,
Cicadas squeak their single monotone.
Poised in the blue heat
The snake darts its tongue,
Squirms deeper into its crevice.
A single, lidless I stares up.

The valley draws in a breath,
Holding it fast as the sun pours
Brassy and bright upon it.
The God moves in the secret places.
Plunging upon the darkness of earth
He wears the look of a guilty son.

Heat yawns and the rocks sweat:
Straining to flow to the cool of night.
The scorpion freezes into stillness,
Cocks his tail in Apollo's eye.

ON VISITING AN
EXHIBITION OF THE GODS

Silent.
    Captured.
Where are your voices?
Not the spirit noise
Piped though vents around us.
Looking in,
    do we listen,
Or do we merely glance
and walk on.
Think upon life and death
Is the injunction.
Do we, or do we move
    Quickly
To less disturbing things?
Leaving,
    I think part
Of my soul remains—briefly—
Considering the voices
That sounded once
In houses long fallen.

Are you aware
Or do you sleep,
Eternally, behind glass?

INVOCATION TO THE OLD ONE

Welcome to you, Old One.
Welcome to the snow and ice,
The bitter cloud of your breath,
The pillow-feathered snow.
Welcome you in, this Winter day.

May your blessing hold us,
May your chills avoid us,
May the bright promise
Of each clear day
Remind us of your gifts.

Old One, cold one
Though we fear your storms,
Yet we welcome you
Into our winter hearts,
With your cleansing breath,
To blow away the old year
And usher in the new.

DARK MOTHER

The dark mother sits in her chair
Adream with silent longing
Though cast in black stone
Her face seems pale
As though her watching
Had clouded her pure dream.

She smiles upon the world with sadness
Her sorrow wrapped in stars—
She bears at her knee the Child
Whose pierced gaze weeps blood.

In her hands she holds, smoothed
By time into a world-shaped globe
A crystal of time as yet unshattered
The stone of forgetting: the dreamstone
Of her unfledged desire.

DARK MOTHER

The dark mother sits in silence
Her dreaming face alight with reflection.
No one will tell her yet
If the dream is realised.

PHILOCTETES ON LEMNOS

To be a poet is to be deserted by one's own kind,
who regard all those of such persuasion
as mad men, charlatans, or freaks.
As Philoctetes who, when he received
the snake bite of the muse,
thereafter could only shout and rave,
at regular intervals, wild agonies of truth—
which, being misconstrued, his fellows
could not bear to hear—and banished him
to Lemnos, without companion, hope, or friend.
From where, despite privation, through which
he grew lank and foul, he continued to loose
from the Bow of Heracles, burning arrows of truth.

CIRCLES

Written at the Stonehenge Exhibition,
The British Museum, 2022.

Dragons' breath on sky stones,
Crowns that tell time in ages
Brown bones, golden capes,
Drums no living child will play.

Over the mound the sun sets,
Stone giants prowl under fading stars,
While Stones that fit the hand precisely
Arm the hunter for the kill.

Driftwood shaped to visions of gods,
Tomb mouths gape under drifting cloud
Swords guard the way
Though hands are long gone.

Stone and wood, shale and bone
Caught by the moment, dissolving

Under shadow and breath,
Give lie to all we think is ours.

No truth here but absolutes,
Wisdom etched in stone and gold
Fired by the light of ages,
Frozen in folds of space.

Nothing else will endure as long
As these gatherings from
Unassailable pasts. We see
But do not see unless we feel.

The breath still stirring in the dusty palm
Show us nothing, but we hear
Bird song and trembling wave,
The heartbeat of a time not lost.

Spears and stones cast adrift.
Cups of Kindness plunged
In seas that remember
The kiss of the keel.

A fragment of cloth, touched once
By hands long dust. It holds
All memories of that fingers touch.
Nothing now is lost. All say: remember.

THE KING BENEATH THE HILL

For Caitlin and for Rosemary.

When the world was still young
And the forests were dark
There came a great king
From Under the Hill.

    The bushes are hung
    With berries so wild
    The mist clinging hard
    To the frosty hillside.

The King he came forth
Clad in armour of gold
He built a great City
That he could then hold

    The bushes are hung
    With berries so wild
    The mist clinging hard

To the frosty hillside.

The world grew to love him
And followed his lead,
But the darkness it knew him
And on him it would feed.

> The bushes are hung
> With berries so wild
> The mist clinging hard
> To the frosty hillside.

For a time he was mighty
And wielded his sword
But the Old Ones grew jealous
And claimed his reward.

> The bushes are hung
> With berries so wild
> The mist clinging hard
> To the frosty hillside.

In darkness and sunlight
The King he went forth
But the dame came to lead him
Back under the earth.

> The bushes are hung
> With berries so wild
> The mist clinging hard
> To the frosty hillside.

The King is asleep now
Under the Hill

Awaiting the days
When he will forfill:

The Dreams of the Kingdom
The Dreams of the Land
The Dreams of the Kingdom
The Dreams of the Land

    The bushes and the briars
    Are hung now with mist,
    The old drams recalling
    The ancient king's tryst.

FLOWER FACE

Llew took up the spear in his left hand,
Flung it with deadly accuracy,
So that it pierced the stone and heart
Of Gronw Pebyr.

Such accuracy, born of certitude,
Comes only to those who have known love—
Who continue to dream of clear shadows
Even after betrayal.

But those who have carried the fiery shield,
Thereafter always hold the knowledge
Of what must be and what denied,
And make a dedication of their death.

But, as Llew Llaw Gyffes,
Empty handed, smiling terribly,
Spurned the corpse of Gronw,
He thought only of her
whose name meant ever 'Flower Face.'

FOUR MINOTAUR POEMS
FOR MICHAEL AYRTON

1: THE MINATOUR SPEAKS

I nuzzle and am held by the dark.
In my cupped hands
a flame of inspired utterance arises.
I am invaded—
and in my endless web of stone
flowers appear and disappear.

The dark flames flicker,
my sight turns inward
and I am freed into a closer prison,
beating on waxen doors
with helpless fists.
Shadows hold me.
I thrust and nuzzle the dark,
and am rewarded by a cry—
my own,
bending round the labyrinth walls.

You! Teacher! Prophet! Seer!
cannot unbind the darkness
that holds me fast;
my cries and bellowings
do not touch your heart.
Only by brute strength, with which,
In a blind moment,
you endowed me
can I batter down these imagined walls.
You shall not hold me.
your dreams will wither,
your mind run down.
I shall be free, you imprisoned
betrayed by your creation
caught in your hollow, dreaming skull.

2: MINOTAUR UNVEILED

These walls thrust me inward
through my blundering shadow
to where I mole-like stumble,
banging my huge and heavy head
against the surfaces from which
my horns strike sparks.
Before me the passageways open—
I feel their pressure on my strange back,
and try to run, falling through darkness,
in search of a chamber in which to hide myself—
wrapped in my own smell.
To hide and be hidden
from the shadow I drag
and the shadows that pursue me;
remembering the hour I confronted

she who held a mirror to my face.

I know the surface of these walls
where I have worn away lifetimes
as perfectly as I know
this appalled splendour rising above my back,
yet now they have become extended
beyond the boundaries of knowledge.
The prison I ransacked for escape
has stretched itself to become
a resting place for gold-pierced dreams.

The walls themselves become mirrors,
where that which I am looks back
daring me to name
what the God has built
between my shoulders
and this terrible head.
I am Icarus also: leaper-towards-the-sun
plunged in the darkest sea.

Risen from the sleep which contains me
I challenge the night;
flying free, my thoughts
burst against the sky-roof of the world,
my bellows echo and re-echo
through a labyrinth of worlds.

3: MINATOUROCRACY

Alone, exploring the maze, I have become trapped,
turning, without Ariadne's red cord,
too many corners that invited me to go

beyond them to the centre's discovery at last.
Now I find myself, no Theseus,
but Asterion rather, humpbacked with shadow
my cries become bull bellowings.

How did this happen? I was certain once
choosing a path with care,
exploring every avenue
until sure it had offered all it could.
Now suddenly I find myself alone.
Someone I knew lead me here.
I was beginning to remember at last.
Without knowing what anything meant
I found myself possessed of certain keys.

Now, calling for Ariadne, for someone to come,
not with a dispassionate sword, but with
the gift of life, or the strong fire of love.
Even the bull must have his rest—
nor yet see his face reflected in the glass.

4: ASTERION'S QUEST

Bull-penned by the Maze,
Asterion walks through mirrored stone,
seeing in himself a changed humanity.
Raging, the monster has become transformed,
laid aside flint hooves for human feet;
couches his back on bitter stone
only that it might grow straight.

In his dream, estranged, groping
for the godhead he endures,

maze-path and mirror-void
show forth his imagining—
dark splendour hooded
under webs of bone
where ghost blood beats.
Slow wings climbing into flight.
he curves a circle in the dark
and in the dream-maze holds
the red birth-cord of his life.

Lost between reflective walls
he sees himself transformed,
each metaphone more human
each bull-mad memory more divine.
Striving to break the carapace of form
he breaks himself, cannot be reborn.

THE GREEN KING

For Peter Neal.

The Green King's a-hunting
Again in the Wildwood
Drawing the swift tracks
Like traces through his hands.

The Green Lord's a-hunting
Again in the Waste
Watching the patterns
Of birds across the sky.

The Green Man's a-rutting
In the ancient mast,
Rooting out the old dreams
From the heart of the Wood.

AND STILL I AM THE GREEN MAN

Under the green woods
I walk alone.
Once all the fields were mine.
And the trees were mine.
The hills
The spired coppices
The straight drills.

Now I must share them
With tractor-stink,
with harvest-slasher.
But I still find ways
To slip the seeds back
Into the furrow,
To watch them grow—
Remembered,
Or forgot.

And still I am the Green Man
And still I walk the fields,

And though the land seems empty
It is filled with life,
And though I am forgotten
I still remember,
And I still watch.

GODODDIN FIELD

All I hear
Is the scream of horses
Falling beneath their riders,
Slain as they were
With Spears and arrows,
With swords of red steel.

How sad it is, how sad
That of all that fell
On Gododdin's field,
They are least remembered:
The bold steeds who
Bore the riders to their deaths.
Both deaths are remembered,
But the horses, dogs, and ravens
Do not forget as they lap
The blood of fallen men.

TROY

After seeing the exhibition at the British Museum, November 2019.

They said there was no Troy
and yet...
here is Troy
spread out before you,
calling your name....

Can you describe it?
stone by stone
rebuild its walls?

Who is that in the shadows?
Achilles, Hector, Andromache?
Not Helen—she is gone
Into myth.
So, who?

Ah...it is you
with all that stolen beauty
anger and war,
you who come here
to the walls
that are not Troy.

THE MAZE-DANCE OF STARS

For Dolores Ashcroft-Nowicki.

I: BEGINNINGS

Through the whorling of stones
beginnings came. We heard them,
voices speaking of the straight track
the maze-way through the wood—
of enormous longings
hunched under hills—
hills always there,
casting shadows on living and dead;
we, childlike, in the face of winter
built our spiral castles—
old power-ways of water and stone.

Who saw us but the stones?
The sky stretched over us

millennia since; constellations
moved across the faces of the gods
like fleeting expressions, while
to the still lakes we came
erecting our houses in the mud.

On the hillside
the dod-man raised his hands
we followed by wood and stream
on tracks of stone, working the pentagrams
of silver and of gold,
shattered by time and hills.
Under the moon
the earth grew slowly silvered,
mists tarnished to ash
the stones crushed to crystal fragments.

Now we moved out of time,
spoke of dreams;
through circling stones
owl and raven, wren and hawk,
hung above bare rocks.
The truth came out of the earth, turning;
a bird's stark cry
left us lonely for our true state—
which is amongst the stars.
There, playing with the white beasts
who came out of mist,
who went in where the earth opened,
we stood at last.

In the Wood again
we saw the light change;

needles pierced our skins
instilling truth like golden rain;
a dagger smoked in a stone trough
and the earth breathed out
the smoke of our dreams.

Kings came after:
to raise the sleeping rock;
lay down in cold beds laughing,
while the wind blew their words,
calling us to rise,
to go forth singing,
to build on other shores.
But nights were long, sleep clinging,
and those who crawled into the cave
in search of fire
came back with wilder words.

Patterns grew out of the dark, changed.
Owls flew out of the night
vanished into day; a sudden burst of light
foretold that in the stones, between the stones
an answer lay—
though none knew what.
Seekers ran to thrust themselves
through cracks in time.
But what came of their action
was the birth of space,
the patterns of law—
great words to conquer the wild waste,
stalking on the dark plain.

We read the crystal pattern in the cup—

crystal grail of circling stars—
we woke at the cauldron's rim,
and walking towards fire and ruin
were turned back by a high winged plover.

Threads of gold patterned the fields,
and on the hill's edge, antlered and shaggy
with beard of mist, a shape moved slowly away,
leaving in its wake a snail-track glimmer
spider-threading a dark world.
The wind unloaded its burden of meaning,
but we could not hear, could not understand,
what was merely an echo among stones.

2: DREAMS

We made a dream of the place only,
not of the people, their needs.
The desires that cut the knot
between hope and belief—
did this too often to understand,
saw only image not truth;
the hawkshead moth alive on dead glass
only an element of escape
evolving from the real reason,
the inescapable,
the mortal.
         Now we began to see
there is more than the desperate sweep
to discover facts, things to fill in
unknown portions of the map.
Before truth became terrible

we sidestepped through shadows,
only to discover that we emerged
into a vacated landscape, treeless and barren,
peopled with ghostly personalities
of those we had made ourselves forget.

Always seeking to be known, to find a face
that did not for once look blankly into
the middle distance, but retained
some awareness of itself—was seen
as part of the new truth we sought.

Often we came to the edge of the circle, of night,
and turned back with cries of longing and loss
as we began to see:
            That there were no familiar roads;
that the stone pillars did not lead, simply,
into the wood, out of the maze;
but were built into the sky itself,
growing out of the oldest earth;
that these were only the first of many gates
that opened, one beyond the other, beyond sight.

We saw only shadows then, as if the image,
struggling to assert its wholeness,
lost faith in existence, became
a word on a page meaning nothing-
and there was nothing to see or understand
except the empty clangor of wind
moaning in the branches of the world.

3: BUILDING

Build a man of circles,
or put stones in the shape of a circle
and you have power and strength.
The circle is there,
a pattern more powerful through which
we may find our route.
              Once,
the patterns were less complex;
now we stand on the brink
of complete understanding,
a bridgeway from one circle to another,
connecting the strands of belief, of law;
defining the bright moats of sun
Through which the leaves of the forest tremble.

Dark, in the turning rim of sun,
we talk of things not understood,
are told to be gentle
but not the meaning of being gentle.
These things seemed too much like dreams—
the circle of mind; the womb;
the circle of destiny; a ship
held in the curve of ocean.
But in the shadows
our hands sometimes touched.

What conceits tell us of the circle
walked by the mind? Shadows.
Again shadows. Time.

Dark flicker of words in the head—
bearing all our senses away.
　　　　On field and hill
the circles are mileposts of our dreams.
They flicker out. Candles. Shadows.
Fragmented as broken bone.

In the circle we come together
mastering individuality. Encompassed
by an overreaching power, a law of changes
and a law of growth.
Stone on stone, endless
the drawn circles of dream.
walking among stars is not enough—
We must be at the making of the stars.

Moving at the edge of the circle, passing inward,
over the rim towards some given point,
we challenge the pattern of defeat,
grow strong in strife and meet
the ancient darkness before which light breaks.
Behind the pattern we assert ourselves,
break all barriers, real or imaginary
between our dreams and their realisation.
Shadows dissolve into clean midnight
in which the moon rides banked cloud
clear into the face of morning.
We feel the sun burn hot across our backs.

4: DANCING

This is the true nature of the dance—
we were not born to sorrow or to die;
all we can ever learn is ours to learn,
all mysteries plumbed, all truths to die
deeper into single truth.

The universe turning round our heads
is no illusion—we grow from the centre,
dance through labyrinths of time and death
to reach the centre—and are reborn.
Sun and moon together fashioned us,
set their marks in heart and mind;
the truth sings to us like a leaping flame,
waiting discovery at the dance's heart .

Poets, lovers, men and gods,
are only names we called ourselves;
older than love, God or poetry,
something moves, half hidden, confusing;
again and again we catch a glimpse,
Only to lose all sight of it.

We are the dancers who see our way
little by little as the maze unfolds,
following the stag of love.
The forest maze
unwinds before us like a veil.
Suddenly we arrive in the secret country,
finding it hauntingly familiar,
peopled with faces we knew,
impossibly, unfathomably, their images reconciled.

The stones turn from us, showing their backs.
Our future is clear: a long procession of days,
where we walk with unicorns,
feed golden lions from our hands.
In perfect truth the land awaits;
Snow melts like flesh from the sleeping beasts.
It is the old story of the wasted land
Of the hidden place we carry in ourselves;
It is the maze unriddled
The worlds of love and hate—
Reconciled.

A cloud had come across the dream,
as we lay sleeping in the lap of time.
Now the cloud has blown away,
the world shines upon us,
life clamours at our eyes and ears.
We are open to receive it,
open to winds of heaven and song of stars.
We, the dancers, dreamers, gods,
put our hands in the fire of earth
and pull forth ourselves grow wise.

5: BREAKING

After the breaking of the pattern
scattered sense of image
caught in a glass. Not lost: potent.
We saw the fish, the star;
The lancepoint indicated truth.

We had moved beyond circles, saw space
curving away into strange distance.

It seemed the barren way might open now;
the flow of images alter.
The dark book lay open,
its pages blank as stone,
a sky washed clean with rain.
Nothing came, no dream
entered where there was but soil long dead.
Erosion entered the mind; the heart grew sick;
we went away again; the world turned.

Men came to break the circle anew;
the stars flamed with renewed fire:
applause for the sanctioned hero.
We made ourselves mazes: dressed our bones
in new flesh: called ourselves
Men and women; danced to the moon;
drew circles in the hard earth.
Laughter entered us;
speech became meaningful;
a new age of dreams began:
half-light spreading over the bridge of sleep,
Leading us along the spiral
To the cave of dreams.

~

Falling back on dreams of perfection,
children in a world-sized wilderness,
we have been so long finding our way.
No one really understood the reasons
for acting as we did—small things
gave rise to endless chances
as we searched for a way home.

That word 'home' came to mean so much.
but did we ever stop to think what it really meant?
There might have been something in the longing
if only we had seen
how much of what we wanted
lay still inside ourselves.

Shadowy world. The city was there,
a looming darkness colouring our lives—
tall towers and green hillsides battled
for each other and for us—the dod-man
raised his fists in rage at last.
But even then we did not see.

Yet in the Wood the other night
when we spoke of the dream again
there seemed a new note.
What was it? Hope? Truth? Shallow words.
But we might try to say, to think
that in all the echoes of our effort
there is at least one constant—
the dark enclave where we walked,
The old Eden where we went last
And may return to, yes may in the end
find our path circular.
And here, before us, the miracle
is reenacted again;
in the neon darkness,
the night-scream of the owl
breaks in upon us like a wave

And, in the shadows, life stirs.
You may say there is nothing left
but a picture hung upon a wall;

but slowly you begin to understand
and are left without breath,
or room to do more than appreciate.

What we are isn't in the cards.
It's forward into an awe-filled world
that beats in upon us, forces us
Out of ourselves into a returning worldscape,
which has become, at last, familiar.

PART TWO
IN ARTHUR'S LAND

HALLOWFLIGHT

Bound under the wing of Summer
For Sarras, splendour of cities,
Galahad lay in the great bed
Under a canopy of red, white, green—
Three colours of the Tree of Life
Which changed with every dream,
From white, paradisal, Virgin,
To green, fecundity of Eve,
To red, blood of Abel's slaughter.
His dream made plain,
The Grail knight slept in memory of peace.

The ship had come from lightning
On a sea of leaden dreams,
beyond expectancy, in prophecy,
The Sibyl's gift from past to present,
From Solomon's city she stretched
Her hand to the hand of Elain,
The Prophetess of the Grail.
Under time's linked banners

The ages grew together, pollarded
By the wood of Eden's gift.

Adrift under Sun's rift
The Grail ship, bound now,
For Sarras, shimmered on the water
Like a gift of sunlight.
The Grail Knight, his dream made plain
Slept in the shadow of the Summer Tree.

MERLIN WAKING

Since I am dreaming here
and since there is nothing new
to dream,
I am content
to set the dream aside,
to open a new door,
to look beyond...

Now that there is nothing
but the mist arising,
and the false dawn,
too loudly filled with birdsong,
I am content
to lay that aside
and to look once more
at the way things were...

And since there is nothing more to say of that
save that I am still tuned
to the soul-notes of Orpheus—

whose disenchanted lyre
wrote such havoc on the world;
and since I am
no longer locked
in a hawthorn tower,
I'm content, at last,
to wind a new thread
into the skein of my lives;
to step forward briefly,
into a new forethought...

And now there is no one
to sing the refrain of my sorrow
and since starlight
placates the wilderness
in which I was born
I am content also,
to put aside memory
to admit I am content.

MERLIN IN CELYDDON

Based on a poem composed by the bard
Myrddin in the 6ʰ century AD.

Bitter and gloomy my time
in the Wood of Celyddon;
snow to my thighs,
icicles in my hair.

Birds sang to me loudly
in the Wood of Celyddon;
no comfort were they
when I thought of my troubles.

Lonely and bitter my time
in the Wood of Celyddon;
the wind howling nightly,
rain falling by day.

Five times four seasons I was
in the Wood of Celyddon;
conversing with creatures
who shared my misfortune.

Madness mastered me
in the Wood of Celyddon;
vision strengthens me
as I depart from the trees.

MERLIN'S CAVE
2005

As if the seas were not enough
The Wind shouts in the cavemouth
Forcing me back out
Into crashing spume.

Old Merlin, I hear your voice
Like stones rolled over by the waves
In the hollow wind—cry
In the waves' complaint.

Echoes of other times—
Children screeching like crows.
Always the crash of waves
Shatters all else to shards.

MORDRED AND THE BIRD

The gold rimmed shadows of falsitude
hung chains of incestuous origin round,
and the Bastard Cruelty of Logres sat, indolent,
by the Tree that signified much more than life.

The red orange yellow green blue spectrum Bird
drew near in lassitude and excression
and out of the puerility of corruption stole a Cat
with velvet fingertips underworn beneath skeletal claws.

The Cat with ineluctable certainty took the light
between its jaws, and beneath the crunch of bones,
the slaver of flesh, the Bastard's low laugh
was a dewdrop in the dying Kingdom.

The bird cried out from surprise at sudden finding
death: 'But I shall return!' and the Cat's twisted stomach
screamed, filled with the lap of waters,
and fear was in Avilion because of that death.

At that sharp prophetic cry
the cruelty of indecisionate decision
was spurned by flesh and came instead to be
like Garlon, indivisible and challenging,

And with a twist of stricken bone,
The bird was gone—and in its place
there wormed a snake
which slowly and prematurely shed its skin:
scattering its incest to the four winds.

FIVE GRAIL SONGS

— I —

This cup
holds light
like liquid fire
burning holes
in the heart.

This icon
signifies
the birth
of truth
in a dead land.

This light
wraps around
the dark
illuminating
everything.

— II —

From the edge of space
light, gathered up,
is centred
into a single drop.

In the Grail,
it blossoms,
becomes more real;
hangs in the treetops

Like a fatherless child,
waiting for someone,
passing,
to take it home.

— III —

I have stood at the table
of the winter king
eaten of the food
set before me;
shared the goodness
that was mine to share.

Wherefore, now,
do I stand
in the cold night
on the wintery moor,
bereft of speech
as the cauldron born.

— IV —

I have tasted
food of the grail.
Fool no more
I woke the world
searching, again,
for the door that opened
once before—
admitting me
to the garden beyond.

— V —

The year turns over
bright light after gold
shafts spring from the Grail
blinding sight.

And we are dazzled
only so that
in the moment we may see
clipped close as a snail

the unfurled pattern of the year:

the Grail will be raised
the Wasteland healed
our part just to wonder
to preserve life's law.

TALIESIN AND RAVEN

Raven has transformed me.
In feather-black I dance
In cloak of dust I dance
In black-wing-rags, I dance.

Raven has remade me.
I see with his eyes
I sense with his senses
I gabble with his beak.

Raven has taken me.
I am shaken by his knowing
By a wisdom older than rock,
By a strength pure as water

By his gift of perception
By his gift of laughter
By his gift of joy.

TALIESIN AND THE SONG OF THE QUEST

Eyes like spears had Taliesin.
From his chair at the head of the hall
He watched gravely the play of the knights.
Once wine had been drunk and food consumed
He laid hands to his wondrous harp-strings
And struck from them a song of wisdom.
In the midst of the carousal he made silence,
And laid forth a song of the subtle Goddess,
Naming her the Friend of Life, and Huntress of the Wood.

To the hushed and waiting throng
He sang the beginning of the Quest.
They heard his words in silence, the famous Bard;
And some smiled in wonder at his song—
They who did not know,
Of his journey to Caer Sidi where
He heard songs of the Noble Head
That told how the Kingdom would fall.

All the while, in the hall of Arthur,
He made songs of warning that went unheard.
Not wise the one who
Scorns the words of a poet
Versed in the wisdom of the Wood,
Whose initiation was before recorded time,
Whose strength was as fire in the blood.

TALIESIN SINGS
OF HIS KNOWLEDGE

Once I knew
Everything there was to know:
In a moment of burning ecstasy
I became transformed,
Knew every rock and tree
Bird, animal, and fish,
And, in a twinkling,
Perceived all meanings to be one.

Then, in just as swift a moment,
From lightnings to returning dark,
I forgot all I had learned.
It was as though, where I had beheld
Only unities, now I beheld,
Only the fragmented moieties
Which once were whole.

Since then, long years of seeking,
Of striving to recover the fragments
Through which I might, somehow,

Put back the broken littoral
Into that same whole
Which is eternal
And does not change.
Only I have changed, become
Frozen in time and space.

Now I look back
At the past and push
The fragments into new patterns,
Eternally hoping to find
Their true relationship,
So that the fire of creation
Might be kindled
In my bones.

TALIESIN TO BEOWULF

Stepping into the worldwood
I found myself in later days
Where men still sang of heroes
And of one great man—Beowulf.
Grim faced, his voice strong,
Of hands mighty, he cut his way
Through paths of blood and bone
To the heart of the dragon,
seeking the hero's gift—
a beast to slay.

TALIESIN'S INVOCATION

I invoke the clash of spears,
The faces of the queen,
The dreams of men.
I invoke the passage of time—
The shuttering and unshuttering of windows.

I invoke the memory of the earth,
The Dreams of the Cymry
The scream that Lludd and Llevellys heard,
The Chessboard of Arthur,
The Cloak of Memory,
The Sword of Forgetting
That must not be drawn.

I invoke the sorrow of the forgotten,
The memory of vision,
The spirit of wonder.
I invoke the song of wisdom
The vision of truth,
And the voice of the Drowned Lands.

I invoke the honour of heroes,
The meeting of two streams—
The Red and the White.
The words of Merlin
The words of Aneurin,
The song of Mabon,
And my own song—
For I am Taliesin still, the Rememberer.
For all of time I stand
Sentinel at the gate of the Otherworld.

I invoke the Branch that whispers,
That sings from the otherworld,
Inviting us to journey there.
I invoke the green and burning tree
That carries the wonder of the Otherworld
From head to heart.

I invoke the threefold death:
The death of time,
The death of memory,
The death of spirit.
And I invoke the threefold journey:
Into knowledge,
Into wisdom,
Into life.

I invoke the starry heavens,
And the paths between.
I invoke the memory of time
The memory of love,
The memory of truth—
For all time.
I invoke memory itself:

The Clash of Spears,
The Faces of the Queen,
The dreams of Little Men.
For I am Taliesin still
Sentinel at the gate...

TRYSTAN AND
THE IRISH QUEEN

T ristan and Iseult, afloat
      on their tideless sea,
      found life and death
in the wine they drank;
and for a moment stood
in an unfamiliar place,
shaded by plane trees,
burned dry by the sun;
shaken by violent storms
or cooled by a yellow moon.

Thus their tragedy—
    that, gifted with the sight
    to see their separate fears and hopes,
    neither had the strength of will
    to change their own estate
    for countries other than they knew—
    and in this way to have dwelt apart
    within the world and yet not of it.

.   .   .

But passion stirred the mud and silt
    until the water darkened—
    and of their dreams
    there only remained for them
    the fall, swiftly or slowly as the world
    might deem, toward their death,
    their final dissolution.

BEFORE CAMLAN

In the Kings court
A single lantern burned,
Holding back the dark.
Taliesin, standing above the gate,
saw the small gleam
And breathed out the words:
"As long as the light burns
Memory enfolds us, truth is held
by the hands of both
The infinite and the earthly Lords."
The King turned, restless in his bed,
As though he felt the words,
Understood their meaning.
Elsewhere, Lancelot, burning
With his own dark light,
Sweated out the dream
He carried eternally within.
Gawain, the blaze of his fires
Dimmed by the darkness,
Paced in his room,

Swearing vengeance for the death,
Of Gareth in the crowded yard.
All these, and the rest,
The Golden courtiers of the Golden court,
Slept or woke or waited.
Only the Kings poet, wakeful, held the gate
And breathed out his greatest fear:
"If all fails tomorrow,
The dream must still survive."
His words, like bright birds, flew
From the gates and outward,
Over the darkened land. Distant,
The moon woke, escaping the cover
Of cloud and, swollen with portent,
Swept across a world,
Yet unprepared for war.

ARTHUR AT THE MERE

— I —

Right at the bottom of the Mere
A light blew back at me there.
It broke across me in a brazen glare
Then suddenly was obscured
By a shadow which a cloud had lured,
And staring up, I saw the light
Was but the sun, And at that sight
My spirit fell and night
Was my bane. Then I looked again
At the water and, like rain,
It glowed and sparkled though there was no sun.
And of a sudden I desired to run,
To be far from that haunted place: have done
With all the Mage's wizard power
And know again sweet freedom for an hour.
But, like a lodestone, it drew my gaze
Glittering and glinting there: the Sword, and it's blaze
The like of which in all my days

Will I never more behold.
Then, doing as I had been told,
I made the barge draw nearer
And there, far from home and wearier
Then I could tell,
I snatched the gift. From where it fell
I knew not then, but felt the cold touch
Of that other hand who's clutch
Had but late possessed the sword.
Without a word
I rowed back to the silent shore—
My hands felt not the roughness of the oar—
And on the land stood he: the Mage,
My friend he said, for all his age—
And yet I feared his grim, grey gaze.
But, I had the sword: mine to hold
And though I shivered with the cold
That came not from the wind,
I knew that never more should I be blind
So long as I held Excalibur; and I signed
To Merlin standing silent there—

That for my life he need no longer care,
For there was not any man would dare
Challenge my right to throne and crown.
He smiled. The sun went down.
And in the Mere I saw the shadows drown.

— II —

Great weight pressed down upon me then
As I came to the steely Mere again,
And the long red grass rippled when
The chill wind blew through it and, as I was laid

71

Beneath a stunted tree, I heard it said
That not a man among my knights had life.
And then I knew the way was rife;
That Guinevere, my queen, my wife
Would find her love in Lancelot, and
That they would walk together on Camelot strand.
I thought then too of Modred, my own son,
On whom the light had never shone,
Whose own dark soul had swiftly gone
When I cleft his helm and knew
That all that I had done was true.
So my knights, but two, laid me beneath the tree—
It was no longer easy to see—
And Excalibur was returned
To the waters that so brightly burned;
And I thought of all that I had learned
Beneath the Mere of old
When I was young, mayhap even bold,
And heard not what Merlin told.
I felt my life grow weak
And knew that I must seek
The way of Kings, the truth behind the lies.
I looked up into the eyes
of honest Bedivere; so a great a size
He seemed to me, and tried to speak—
But found no sound would break
From out my lips. So I signed to them then
That my journey should begin,
And felt my heart knocking within.
The barge came close across the Mere—
I could see it there—
And knew that I would waken soon
On the Isle beneath the moon,
Ruled by three Queens in all their bloom;

And all in peace beneath the flowering thorn
Where all the joys and sorrows of kings are born,
Would rest my head
On the soft deep rushy bed,
And pass beyond the mournful care
Of all—even so to lie there
'Til the day arises like a spirited mare
And thunders out a brassy call
That shall echo in every hall,
Setting free the winds of earth
Planting anew the seeds of mirth
And shaking the things of greatest worth—
Until I, maybe, shall walk as once before
Upon the wakening shore.

ARTHUR IN THE CURVE OF TIME

Through the rain of time
Arthur heard the voice of guns.
He turned his head a little,
listening, his hands wrapped
close about his wine cup
as though it were a grail.

The wind whipped wet and weeping
against the elevated windows;
Arthur's hands, shaking, spilled
drops of red wine, that soaked
like blood into the white fur
drifting snowy to his feet.

Unnoticed, he left the wine
And crept like a ghost
through his own world—
and found that such he was.

THE KING'S MOON-RITE

For David Jones.

From the mounds of Crooked Bank there came
but three common men: Morvran mab Tegid,
who for his ugliness no man would strike;
Sendaf Bright-Angel, who for his beauty
death forfend; and Glewelwyd Mighty-Grasp
whose strength none might withstand...

These three through the field walked arm in arm
as Logres-in-Britain crumbled into darkness once again,
and once again dreams rode the land—
of the man who struck the Grievous Blow
(the Red Man from the Lake)
and he who forbore to ask the Question;
and of the Ship of Glass that never sailed
but rode the shape of Bardsey—
while the Bear went out in Prydwen
to rifle Hell and come again
with gifts for all who still held true...

He is remembered in the stars—Arcturus and Telyn Idris—
and the mountains do not forget
the debt of Crooked Bank.
But the head of Bran no longer stares above Lud's Town
and Caer Siddi is renamed Grassholm to our loss.
Nor is it known who lay in need: King Pelham,
Lord of Lystenesse, or the Crow with the Singing Head.

But She who waits beyond the water, watches still,
crooning to her poet-lover, caught within the bush,
and dreams her long dream into night.
And who has seen her floating on the water's moonlit silver
that has not also heard her siren song
mazing both mind and heart?

And who has seen the Cup flame in the West
that has not also seen the breath of Nine
smoke on the air to warm the Cauldrons rim?
And who has seen the Table, that has not seen it crack
as men rode over it with plunging hooves
to scatter the titled chairs in which the hosts had sat?

The Sword went down in water, shaken and drowned
by the white hand rising from the depth.
The Sword was named Escalibor, the Spear Rhongomyniad,
the Mantle of brightness Gwern...
lost to the beating heart of life.

But he who was both Lord and King,
Dux, Director of Toil, Amherawdr,
the Lord of the Wave in ancestral purple walking in the Waste
sits yet upon his golden chair, his hair and beard grown long,
and in the cave he sleeps, the Great Bear, the Crow,

and leads the Hounds of Annwn over height of moor and peak
and casts a silver horseshoe on Sant John's Eve,
and guards the Burning Tree for better days.

THE LADY OF THE LAKE

The hawthorn flowers again
And the land is green,
But she lies alone in her tower
Awaiting the word that will free her
Into the world she has lost.

So long divided, so long
Forced to follow the path of denial:
She had thought only death
Could free her from her savage cell.

Now, as the year turns over,
As the hawthorn flowers again,
She hears the words of freedom
Spoken by one late-coming to her land.

At once, her chains unbound,
she feels her heart's sweet blood
Beating in the land.

With joyful singing
She sends her blessing forth upon the wind.

MYSTERIES OF THE GRAIL

The dead King lies in the perilous bed
Uncorrupt, his soul caught in a wrack of air,
His hands folded in a long dream of day.

The Grail Knight, distant, wrought of clay
Dreams of a King whose wounds will never heal
Unless the Cup is brought to birth.

In the silence of the dark earth
The waters stir to life
The King's hands wake and move.

The hands of the Knight eschew strife;
He holds the sword from the red stone
And wields the bonds of love.

The neophytes who watched the sky above
The Castle of the Grail, awake
To see the Mystery complete.

PART THREE
IN MYTH'S GREAT HEART

THE SHIP OF FOOLS,
THE DANCE OF DEATH

In tutina mentis dubia
fluctuant contraria
lacivus amor et puditicia.
sad sligo quad video,
collum iugo prebeo;
ad ingum tamen suave transeo.
—Carmina Burana

— I —

A Great Wheel lies across the sun,
of fifteen spokes,
and at the foot of each there lie
those who have walked on earth,
those who have died and found their way
to wisdom's cold dark shore;
whose faces, carved in stone,
smile upon those who walk below
seeking the gates of Paradise.
Angel and Devil guard these gates,

turning the wheel through time's long day and night;
all but a privileged few are turned aside
and cast upon the blood red sea—
a Ship of Fools to ply their course
in search of their own dark destiny.
Others pass within to learn
the secrets of the endless dance;
to find the hidden flower at the Maze's heart,
and wake with Love's enduring chords
flooding their opened minds.

— II —

The ship sails on, its crew grown merry.
In time their laughter gains a hollow ring,
and under the stormcloud's leaden eye
trees lean on one another,
their branches claws that grasp the air,
twisting to swing the skulls of long dead kings
left hanging in an open mouth of sky.
These were pure men once, with lightened ways,
who walked in the morning light of day, or danced,
and did not care for thoughts of death—
but Death is a dancer too,
and draws in everyone,
and on his ship these fools must sail
between the frowning faces of the sun and moon.

— III —

A Dreamer came this way, with word of dream.
He sang a song of sin and death,
making them cheerful things-
then tore his own heart from his breast

and tossed it, bleeding, at our feet.
But this was in the days before the Dance began
And we, who once were mild and sweet,
Threw off our smiling masks and wept.
And after that, with cries and screams,
the dancers of the Horned One strong came on.
We watched them in the sudden-coming night
their faces painted white, with staring eyes.
Their bones stuck through their sudden robes,
and yet they sang with heaven's voice of gold.
Bones of kings they picked from off the ground,
tossed up crown and robe, and dressed themselves in gold;
clawed their painted faces till the blood ran down,
and screamed with laughter at the corpses in the snow.
Under their stamping feet the earth grew still,
the stones themselves turned white with winter's death.
No part of life those frozen faces,
posturing hands and frantic limbs—
but they had danced the Dance of Death
into the Dance of Spring,
And young men's voices echoed at the gate again.
In the morning there was song through all the fields of men,
as they woke in the shadow of the open gate
and saw the green land stretching into night,
and how the silver knight held out a mail-clad hand
and how his gentle lady lay her own in his.
Death the puppet primped before a mirror,
painting his eyes and lips before the dance.
And back-to-back the Angel and the Devil danced,
bound by ropes of love and fear.
But Death was defeated by a lover's kiss
and man with woman danced, touching lip to lip,
until the Goddess in her golden car came by,
offering to her God-in-Man

an apple of the sun to bite,
and down-turned corners of old age's mouth
were seen to be the other face of youth and love.

— IV —

There were two lovers in the spring of life
who vowed to love forever and be true—
they lie in silent ardour now, faces carved in stone;
and only in the poet's rhyme
do their hands reach out to ever intertwine.
Love is our Lord, undefeated by death;
our fate is to be always alone
to hear the storms of life go by
and sing sweet songs of nothingness.
We had a choice once, long ago,
between the light and dark,
bright passion or the whitest robe;
now we sail this boat of fate
beneath a canopy of singing stars.
The body is the battleground of life,
seeking a victory for love and truth;
words have gone wild in the poet's mouth
to answer the riddle of the knot of Time.
We had a choice once, long ago,
but followed the inclination of the road,
which led us to the endless sea,
and set us adrift to find our way.
Now we sing of all life's pleasures,
caught in a hungry net,
and still we cannot choose a way
above the rising clamour of the wind and wave.
Love is Our Lady, fortune's Goddess,
her body white as snow;

her smile can break the stars from bud,
her frown break a soul in two.

— V —

Wild the dance, and long the love,
But we were made to be that way,
shining bodies, glorious to see,
faces of carven beauty.
You have nothing to fear—
only the truly dead are cast adrift
as we were, long ago,
To sail the flood forever
in a boat of faithless fools.
Those who see and come to dance with us
(alone in the Wasteland, dancing in a circle)
are freed forever from the curse of time,
and stay with us forever, 'til the dawn.
Wake! Wake! Good people, wake!
The night of death is passed again,
Love's morning dawns upon the fields.
The smiling face looks down
eyes closed not by blindness but in ecstasy.
Wake! And discover you are not really dead;
understand the piercing sadness of the night
that gives way to a joy-filled day.
Whatever you were made for, you are right for this.
Rejoice! The dawn is breaking,
Night's toys are put away.
We are fools together in the light of day,
only in the night set free to find our way
back beyond the start of Time
to our first days of mortal birth.
And all this may happen again tomorrow,

as once again the Ship of Fools sets sail,
Ploughing her ancient furrow through the waves.
Turning in the endless circle of the dead we find
The Wheel contains all men and women, all kinds;
And wisdom is a circle too, and moves
Between the setting of ther Sun and Moon.
Then: be birds, be beasts, men or gods become.
Fly as you would fly, sing, jest, make love—
lest he who says another word find out,
the Devil dances to our flutesong too.

— VI —

This is the true nature of the dance:
we were not born to sorrow or to die
but lie in fields of clover, watching birds fly.
All the joy we know becomes Godlike,
born of love and friendship,
and the long study towards understanding
our place among the stars.
The universe turning round our heads
is no illusion—we grow from the centre,
dance through labyrinths of time and death
to reach the centre, and are reborn;
tossed among the tangle of lover's limbs
we smile and grow golden,
and are streaked with silver fire.
Sun and moon together fashioned us
And set their marks in heart and mind.
Love's glorious fire, and Death's ashy pyre—
we were made for both,
and the truth sings in us like a leaping flame
waiting discovery at the dance's heart.
All knowledge lies open to us—

till we face the sun, the moon, as equals
brother and sister, smiling with us
at the shadow-ghost of Time.
Poets, lovers, men and gods,
are only names we have called ourselves.
Older than love, Gods or poetry,
something moves, half hidden.
Again and again we catch a glimpse,
only to lose all sight of it.
This makes mock of all our dreams
For it is the secret at the heart of everything—
that makes death seem
no more than the indrawn breath
life just now exhaled.
We are the dancers who see our way
little by little as the Maze unfolds;
we follow the stag of love,
and the forest maze of trees
winds back from our eyes like a veil.
Suddenly we arrive in a secret country
And find it hauntingly familiar,
Peopled with faces of those we knew and loved,
Impossibly, unfathomably, their images reconciled.
The Wheel turns round us
and suddenly our heritage is clear—
the days when we walked with Unicorns
and fed the Golden Lion from our hands.
In perfect truth, the land awakes,
snow melts like flesh and beasts awaken.
It is the old story of the Wasted Land again,
of the hidden place we carry in ourselves;
it is the Maze at last unriddled,
the worlds of love and hate,
reconciled, reconciled!

A cloud fell across the Dream,
as we lay sleeping
with our heads in the lap of Time.
Now the cloud is blown away
and the world shines out upon us
in all its brightest array.
Truth clamours at our eyes and ears
and we are open to hear it—
open to the winds of heaven and the song of stars.

And we: the dancers, the dreamers, the gods,
put our hands into the fire of earth
and pull forth ourselves grown wise.

ῙMMRAMA · ẆANDERINGS

Inspired by the ancient Irish tale of the Voyage of Maelduin.

THE ISLE OF VOICES

For days our keel
sliced through the black sea,
then suddenly before us
an island rising like a fist.
As we came to shore
drawn by the tide's secret hands,
we saw a crowd emerging from the rocks
who, when they saw us,
began to make such noise
It was a while before we understood their words.
"It is they!" we heard, "It is they!"
Fear spread through us as we listened,
but before we could learn what this might mean
a wind sprang up, filling our sails,
and swiftly the island fell astern.

Yet it seemed we still could hear,
distant on the chill air:
"It is they, they, they!"

THE ISLAND OF LAUGHTER

The voyage was long, and we grew tired.
Then at noon we espied a new island,
a flat and grassy shore with low green hills
and distant clustering houses.
Along the shore and inland we could see
groups of fair people, laughing and dancing.
Eagerly, we pressed forward,
but caution ruled our captain
and only one, chosen by lot, we sent ashore.

Immediately he joined the play; he who been,
a moment before, weary
and was, by nature, sad,
now gave vent to mirth and pleasure.
In wonder we watched him,
greeting folk as though he knew them well,
and felt the sorrow of those
who know too much of laughter.

Grimly we turned our craft about
and left the shore and our fellow
to what we thought must be
unending merriment. Behind us,
as dusk fell, we heard laughter and shouting still,
that followed us on the clear air.

THE ISLAND OF GOD'S TREES

On the next island we met a man,
ancient as care, who told us how,
when a youth, he had set sail,
following the sea's green road
in search of God. But his boat
had begun to tremble, though the sea
remained flat calm, and so returning
to land, he cut four squares of turf
to steady the rocking of his craft.

Thereafter he sailed on easily
until, reaching this spot
on the open sea, his boat
would sail no further.
Then, God himself appeared
(the old man could give us
no description)
and set the strips of turf
side by side on the open sea,

'Each year since then,'
he told us with pride,
'God has added
another foot to this island;
and with each foot a tree;
and in each tree are birds—
the souls of those who died
after I left the shores of my country.
These God himself sends to me.'

We smiled among ourselves at this,
but the old man seemed harmless,
and next day, after we had eaten,
taking care not to disturb
the birds that roosted in the trees,
we left his island and sailed on—
only once looking back
to watch it sink quietly in mist.

THE ISLAND OF HORSEMEN

Our ship danced across the waves
as though eager to reach new land;
and soon we sighted an island where
waves ran in upon its shore,
each racing its fellow as if it would be first.

Two of our number went ashore,
bringing back strange tidings;
of cups the size of cooking vats
and huge hammers like young trees—
though God be thanked no sign
of those who owned these things.

When we had taken on water
we did not linger... but as we sailed away
there came to our ears fierce crying,
and over the waves, on horses of fire,
came seven men, taller than trees and mighty.

We could scarcely see them
so great were the clouds of steam they raised,
and in fear lest they had seen us

we waited, watched as they rode ashore
and in wild mad clamour began to race
about and about the island shore.

For a time, we watched in wonder,
as they showed no sign of tiring,
and when at last we sailed away
they still rode their furious steeds,
as though to cool them—
or in quest of an unknown prize.

THE ISLAND OF THE BLACK AND WHITE SHEEP

He stood on the middle line
of the island, where a bronze wall
divided it, separating the sheep
into flocks of white and black.
And if he put a sheep that was white
on one side, it was black;
and if he put a sheep that was black
on the other side, it was white.
And he himself was neither black nor white,
but betook a little of that colour on that day.

THE ISLAND OF THE CAT

Who has taken what is not rightly his
must expect to pay the price,
even after dining on roasted ox,
seated on cushions of finest down.
For the Cat watches all that you do
From the four stone pillars
on which he makes quick play;

and if you dare steal from his hoard,
no matter how small the thing,
the Cat will leap through you
like a flaming sword—and sweep
your foolish ashes from the hall.

THE ISLAND OF WEEPING

Hither and thither and to and fro
they went, and all were weeping—
for what cause we could not tell;
and when one of our number went ashore,
he too began to wail and cry
for no apparent reason.
Two others followed,
who were also stricken;
and only after we had sent four more
to fetch them, who would look at nothing
and covered their mouths from the air of that place,
were our fellows recovered.
Nor could they remember
what had made them weep.

THE PILLAR

Sailing in my ship of glass
I came upon a pillar
stretching into the sky
far above me, and sinking
deep into the sea beneath.
And from the height
a mighty net hung down,
through a single mesh of which

I sailed, and as I passed
struck at it with my sword.

It would not break,
and from above,
in the sky it seemed,
a voice, high and clear
and cold as stone, spoke.
But I could not understand
the words it uttered—
and so sailed on, dreaming
of the woman whose wisdom
alone could explain these things.

THE ISLAND OF YOUTH

The third from last island
at the end of the world
was green and shadowed deeply with trees.
There the fabled unicorn ran free
and maidens fairer than jewels
came offering fruit and wine;
and in a pool of clear water
where we bathed,
those who were aged found youth again.

Long days we spent there,
Lost to the voyage, 'til one morning,
inexplicably, the dream passed
like a shiver across the skin,
and we woke on our ship once more,
water sliding beneath its lively keel.

THE ISLAND OF FIRE

On Monday we came to an island
surrounded by a flaming wall
that turned and turned about.
And in the wall a door,
and through the door a glimpse
of people: beautiful, abundant,
happy in their feasting.
But, though strange to say
we felt no heat as we approached,
the wheel of fire defeated us;
and our eyes strained back
with longing as we sailed away,
knowing the desire of those
who see the unattainable
but dare not face the pain.

THE ISLAND OF FIRE PIGS AND ICE BIRDS

In the garden of she who,
it might be,
could explain these things,
lie orchard upon orchard
of apple trees
on which the fruit is all of gold.

There, two things you may see;
the first, a hundred fiery pigs who,
gathering round the trees,
one after the other rush backwards against them,
shaking down the fruit
on which they gorge themselves throughout the day.

Until, when night has almost fallen, the second thing occurs!
Flock after flock of birds,
transparent and glittering like ice,
swim from the shore
towards where the sun begins to set
and, once it has gone from sight, return—
rising from the water
as though it can no longer hold them.
Settling amongst the trees
they devour those apples left by the fiery pigs.

And these things happen every day;
yet always by morning
the orchards are replenished.
And these things happen on her island
who, it might be, could explain everything
—if so she chose;
and I have seen it all
who was on that voyage.

LOTHLÓRIEN

The trees give up their fallow gold,
As leaves drift down from Nimrodell;
The sound of singing, fair and sad
Drifts yet among the trees.

This is the pool of moving stillness.
Under these boughs time waits.
For those who walk here
Are conversant with sorrow.

Sorrows that hover on the tongue,
That remain always inseparable,
Hidden in golden reaches
From memory of other days.

Here there are no dream,
For this is the Great Dream,
The perfect imperfection
The strongest thought.

Here are shifting shoals of light,
Stretched out in lines of sun
Falling, falling, sliding through leaves
Glimmering like iridescent pearls.

Here, between the Mallorn Trees
Where *elanor* and *niphredil* grow
On green grass, in fair Lothlórien
Is the centre of a secret life.

Those who walk here
May not come again,
But ever bear bright Lorien
In the hidden cave of light.

CHAMBER OF STARS

For C of 35 Years.

The Singer of Stars stands still
In the Chamber of Eternal Song
And whispers the Songs of Night and Day
Into the spaces between the worlds,
Where walkers of will emerge
Into the spaces between the leaves
Where starry records keep
The wisdom of the wisest stars.

Ages and aeons pass
As notes of wisdom fall
Into and though the median of time,
Intersecting only once
In the Chambers of the Sun.

Rays fall now, piercing the dark
And tears of starlight drop
Transforming the darker shafts of life

In which the Singer sees
The secrets of the Starry Dome.

Wizards of the Soul have sung
Such songs of bright remembering
That piece the clouds of doubtful rain
And break upon the earth below.
We stand at a place of turning,
Open-hearted with anticipation
Of changes yet to come;
Life's blessings hold us
In glorious bonds of light.

BLAKE'S JOURNEY

My body blows in the wind
Like a corpse hung at a crossroads.
I have seen too much,
Too much, too much
To not know the way
The hanging branch,
The billowing corn,
The Holy Golden wheat
Sings in the Palace of the Mind.
Sings in the mind's holding cell,
The Cupboard of Eternity,
Where the ghosts of today
Run wild in the glowing hearts
Of Poets and Seers.

Do you not hear
The singing winds
That catch
In the falling starry river
The pieces of our Souls

That remember?

My body blows in the wind
Like dandelion clocks,
Twirls in the air
Like ashen keys,
Remembers voyages
From Heart to Head
From Head to Heart
Till making's end.

MYTHDREAMS

Mythdreams in the head
Shatter all complacence.
We become hill-walkers
Shadow dwellers
On the edge of Otherworld.

Mind-dreams in the body
Run through us like
Swords of true light—
We are bound by a promise
Too terrible to ignore.

But the darkest myths
Speak through the blood,
Willing us remember
The shadow-world exploding
In shards of light.

And that paradox

Holds us ambered
Until there is no time,
And we fall
Through our dreams
Into the fullness of life.

POETRY, YOU

For Caitlín.

You who *are* poetry
Need it not.
Close as I seek the mystery
I find you come before.
So, as I work inward
You greet me everywhere.

www.ingramcontent.com/pod-product-compliance
Lightning Source LLC
Chambersburg PA
CBHW032110010726
47493CB00008B/2525